W9-AKC-470

Look Out, Mouse!

Look Out, Mouse!

by **Steve Björkman**

Holiday House / New York

Library of Congress Cataloging-in-Publication Data
Björkman, Steve, author, illustrator.
Look out, Mouse! / by Steve Björkman. — First edition.
pages cm. — (I like to read)
Summary: When Farmer Fred forgets to feed the horse,
the mouse helps out and later, when the mouse is
in trouble, the horse repays his kindness.
ISBN 978-0-8234-2953-0 (hardcover)
[1. Horses—Fiction. 2. Mice—Fiction.
3. Farm life—Fiction.
4. Helpfulness—Fiction.] I. Title.
PZ7.B528615Loo 2015
[E]—dc23
2014006416

ISBN 978-0-8234-3397-1 (paperback)

For Kacie
and Ethan

It is dinnertime on the farm.

But Farmer Fred forgot
to feed the horse!

The mouse
nibbles and
nibbles.

Look out, mouse!
Here comes
the cat!

Look out, mouse!
Here comes
the snake!

Look out, mouse!
Here comes the owl!

Look out, mouse!
Here comes
the weasel!

Look out!
The fox is
coming too!

Look out, mouse!

The horse
neighs.
The dog barks.
The chickens
cluck.

Farmer Fred wakes up.
"What is going on out here?"

It is dinnertime
for the mouse.
Look out, house!

You will like these too!

Come Back, Ben by Ann Hassett and John Hassett
A *Kirkus Reviews* Best Book

Dinosaurs Don't, Dinosaurs Do by Steve Björkman
A Notable Social Studies Trade Book for Young People
An IRA/CBC Children's Choice

Fish Had a Wish by Michael Garland
A *Kirkus Reviews* Best Book
and Top 25 Children's Book

The Fly Flew In by David Catrow
An IRA/CBC Children's Choice
Maryland Blue Crab Young Reader Award Winner

Late Nate in a Race by Emily Arnold McCully
A Bank Street College Best Children's Book of the Year

Look! by Ted Lewin
Correll Book Award for Excellence
in Early Childhood Informational Text

Mice on Ice by Rebecca Emberley and Ed Emberley
A Bank Street College Best Children's Book of the Year
An IRA/CBC Children's Choice

Pig Has a Plan by Ethan Long
An IRA/CBC Children's Choice

See Me Dig by Paul Meisel
A *Kirkus Reviews* Best Book

See Me Run by Paul Meisel
A Theodor Seuss Geisel Award Honor Book
An ALA Notable Children's Book

You Can Do It! by Betsy Lewin
A Bank Street College Outstanding Children's Book

See more I Like to Read® books.
Go to www.holidayhouse.com/I-Like-to-Read/